Snow White

As told by

CATHERINE HELLER

Illustrated by Karen Stolper

Here is Snow White's version of this famous story
Turn the book over and read the story from her stepmother's point of view

A Birch Lane Press Book
Published by Carol Publishing Group

A Birch Lane Press Book
Published by Carol Publishing Group
Birch Lane Press is a registered trademark of Carol Communications, Inc.
Editorial Offices: 600 Madison Avenue, New York, N.Y. 10022
Sales and Distribution Offices: 120 Enterprise Avenue, Secaucus, N.J. 07094
In Canada: Canadian Manda Group, One Atlantic Avenue, Suite 105,
Toronto, Ontario M6K 3E7
Queries regarding rights and permissions should be addressed to
Carol Publishing Group, 600 Madison Avenue, New York, N.Y. 10022

Carol Publishing Group books are available at special discounts for bulk purchases,
sales promotion, fund-raising, or educational purposes.
Special editions can be created to specifications. For details, contact:
Special Sales Department, Carol Publishing Group,
120 Enterprise Avenue, Secaucus, N.J. 07094

Manufactured in the United States of America
10 9 8 7 6 5 4 3 2 1

Library of Congress Cataloging-in-Publication Data

Heller, Catherine.
   Snow White : the untold story / Catherine Heller ; illustrated by
Karen Stolper.
      p.   cm. — (Upside down tales)
   "A Birch Lane Press book."
   Titles from separate title pages; works issued back-to-back and
inverted.
   Summary: After reading the classic tale of Snow White, the reader
is invited to turn the book upside-down and read an updated version
told from the stepmother's point of view.
   ISBN 1–55972–326–2 (hc)
   1. Upside-down books—Specimens. [1. Fairy tales. 2. Folklore—
Germany.   3. Upside-down books.   4. Toy and movable books.]
I. Stolper, Karen, ill.   II. Snow White and the seven dwarfs.
English. III. Title. IV. Series.
PZ8.H3685Sn 1995
398.2'0943'02—dc20
[E]   95–19221
                                                                  CIP
                                                                   AC

Snow White

Once upon a time a good queen sat sewing by a window on a snowy afternoon. When she looked up to see a raven fly away she accidentally pricked her finger and a drop of blood appeared. Oh, how I wish I had a daughter with skin as white as snow, she thought, with lips as red as blood, and hair as black as a raven's wing.

In due time the queen gave birth to such a child, whom she named Snow White. Sadly the queen died soon after Snow White's birth.

The king thought his baby girl needed a mother and soon married again. Although the new queen was beautiful, she was mean, selfish, and very vain. She was able to perform evil magic and spent hours looking at herself in her magic mirror and asking:

> *Mirror, mirror, on the wall*
> *Who's the fairest one of all?*

The mirror would answer:

> *O, Queen, thou hast a beauty so rare*
> *None to thee can compare.*

And the queen was happy.

The jealous queen gave Snow White rags to wear and made her work long hours at hard tasks. In spite of the queen's cruel treatment, Snow White grew more and more beautiful every day. Her sweet and kind disposition made her appear even more lovely, and her goodness shone through on her face. Finally one fateful day the queen asked her mirror:

> *Mirror, mirror, on the wall*
> *Who's the fairest one of all?*

The mirror answered:

> *I speak only truth*
> *Of what is right*
> *The fairest of all*
> *Is the Princess Snow White*

The queen flew into a terrible rage. Snow White? More beautiful than she? The queen would not rest until she was again the fairest in the land! She called her faithful huntsman to her and told him to take Snow White deep into the woods and kill her. To make sure that the deed would be done, she gave him a little box in which to bring back Snow White's heart.

The huntsman told Snow White they were going deep into the woods to pick some flowers. He raised his knife once her back was turned, but he could not bear to hurt her. She turned around, frightened and confused when she saw the knife. "Run away, Princess," the huntsman cried. "I cannot obey the queen and kill you!"

Snow White ran sobbing into the forest. She was hungry and alone and had no place to stay, but even the wild animals recognized her goodness and beauty. They would not harm her and instead led her through the dark night to a bright little cottage. She arrived there just as dawn was breaking.

The cottage was the home of seven dwarfs, who mined gold and jewels in the mountains. They had already left for work when Snow White arrived. She was tired but relieved to find a safe place. Grateful for shelter, she tidied up the messy house and ate a little food she found. Then she fell into a deep, restful sleep across the seven little beds.

Snow White awoke to see seven little men peering at her. They were not used to visitors, much less such a beautiful and sweet one. "Who are you and how did you get here?" they demanded. When they heard the story of the queen's wickedness, they vowed to keep Snow White safe with them. They spent a cozy evening together, happy that they had found each other.

The dwarfs had to go to the mine again early the next morning. They warned Snow White not to open the door to anyone while they were gone.

Meanwhile, the huntsman returned to the castle. On his way back, he killed a wild boar and took its heart back to the queen, so she would believe that Snow White was dead.

The queen was delighted and ate the heart for dinner. But early the next morning she asked her mirror:

> *Mirror, mirror, on the wall*
> *Who is the fairest one of all?*

The mirror answered:

> *Deep in the woods*
> *In a cottage so small*
> *There lives the fairest one of all*
> *As a guest of the dwarfs*
> *She does abide*
> *Princess Snow White is still alive*

The queen was beside herself with anger. She killed the huntsman for his treachery and concocted another evil plan immediately. She disguised herself as an old woman and made a delicious-looking poison apple. Then she set out for the dwarfs' cottage. When she arrived, she heard Snow White happily singing and cleaning inside. She rapped on the door and called out, "Open up, my dear. I have brought you something good to eat!"

"I'm sorry," replied Snow White. "I promised the dwarfs I wouldn't open the door for anyone."

The queen ran to the window. "Look what I have for you, my dear. It would make me so happy to give you this perfect apple as a gift," she cackled.

Snow White did not want to be rude. She did not open the door, but she took a bite of the apple that the old lady had placed on the windowsill. She immediately swooned and fell down as if dead. The queen sped happily back to her castle.

The dwarfs arrived home and were brokenhearted to find their beloved Snow White lying on the floor. They wept and mourned but realized they would now have to live without her. Her skin was still as white as snow, her lips as red as blood, and her hair as dark as a raven's wing. She was so beautiful that they could not bear to bury her in the ground. They made her a clear glass coffin and trimmed it with gold letters that read PRINCESS SNOW WHITE. They set the coffin in a lovely part of the woods and one dwarf always stood guard. Even the wild animals would come to see the beautiful princess.

One day Prince Charming rode by and was over-
whelmed by Snow White's beauty. He listened to the dwarfs
speak of her kindness. He begged them to let him buy the
coffin and its contents for gold, but the dwarfs refused.
So he sat down beside his princess with such longing that
the dwarfs recognized true love. They allowed him to take
the coffin away with him.

While the dwarfs were helping Prince Charming put
Snow White in his carriage, the piece of apple in her mouth
was dislodged and the princess opened her eyes and pushed
up the cover of the case she had rested in. "Where am I?"
she asked.

"You are with me," said the prince. He told her how he
had fallen in love because of her beauty and now wished to
stay with her because of her goodness and kindness. They
planned to be married and set off together for the prince's
castle, promising the dwarfs they would visit often.

The wicked queen had enjoyed a time of contentment with her mirror. But the morning came when she asked:

Mirror, mirror, on the wall
Who is the fairest one of all?

The mirror answered her:

From the sleep of death she has awoke
And with her true love she has spoke
With lips like blood and hair like night
The fairest again is Princess Snow White

Snow White? Still alive? Never was anyone as angry as the queen. She could not even bear to think that Snow White was alive! She smashed the mirror to a thousand bits, but the pieces flew up and cut her to death. Now she could never hurt Snow White or anyone else, ever again.

Snow White and her prince married and lived happily ever after.

That's the story of Snow White that you've probably heard before. But did you know that the queen, Snow White's stepmother, has a different way of telling it? Turn the book over to hear her story.

The Untold Story
of
Snow White

CATHERINE HELLER

Illustrated by Karen Stolper

Here is Snow White's stepmother's version of this famous story
Turn the book over and read the story from Snow White's point of view

A Birch Lane Press Book
Published by Carol Publishing Group

A Birch Lane Press Book
Published by Carol Publishing Group
Birch Lane Press is a registered trademark of Carol Communications, Inc.
Editorial Offices: 600 Madison Avenue, New York, N.Y. 10022
Sales and Distribution Offices: 120 Enterprise Avenue, Secaucus, N.J. 07094
In Canada: Canadian Manda Group, One Atlantic Avenue, Suite 105,
Toronto, Ontario M6K 3E7
Queries regarding rights and permissions should be addressed to
Carol Publishing Group, 600 Madison Avenue, New York, N.Y. 10022

Carol Publishing Group books are available at special discounts for bulk purchases,
sales promotion, fund-raising, or educational purposes.
Special editions can be created to specifications. For details, contact:
Special Sales Department, Carol Publishing Group,
120 Enterprise Avenue, Secaucus, N.J. 07094

Manufactured in the United States of America
10 9 8 7 6 5 4 3 2 1

Library of Congress Cataloging-in-Publication Data

Heller, Catherine.
     Snow White : the untold story / Catherine Heller ; illustrated by
Karen Stolper.
          p.   cm. — (Upside down tales)
     "A Birch Lane Press book."
     Titles from separate title pages; works issued back-to-back and
inverted.
     Summary: After reading the classic tale of Snow White, the reader
is invited to turn the book upside-down and read an updated version
told from the stepmother's point of view.
     ISBN 1–55972–326–2 (hc)
     1. Upside-down books—Specimens. [1. Fairy tales. 2. Folklore—
Germany.   3. Upside-down books.   4. Toy and movable books.]
I. Stolper, Karen, ill.   II. Snow White and the seven dwarfs.
English. III. Title. IV. Series.
PZ8.H3685Sn 1995
398.2'0943'02—dc20
[E]   95–19221
                                                                CIP
                                                                 AC

The Untold Story
of
Snow White

Now, I know you've all been told of how evil and mean I was to my stepdaughter, Blanche, who called herself "Snow White." But that's not the true story at all.

It was very sad when Blanche's mother died. Perhaps to make up for it, her father spoiled her and let her have her way with anything she wanted. She decided on her own clothes, food, bedtime, toys, ponies...anything she wanted! She was nasty to all the servants who wanted to help her. She was even mean to the dogs who lived around the castle.

A princess should set a good example for the other girls in the kingdom. When I married Blanche's father, I knew how important it was for his daughter to look and behave in a respectable way.

I knew that being her stepmother wouldn't be easy. I didn't expect her to love me like a mother, but I hoped we would get along. We both cared for her father, but that didn't turn out to be enough.

Before I became queen I worked selling cosmetics. Naturally I had a good supply of many different products. When I moved into the castle, I brought my special three-way mirror along. When Blanche was little, she used to call it my "magic mirror" and would gaze into it endlessly. As she grew, she became more and more interested in my things.

At first I shared my makeup and mirror with Blanche and gave her some samples of her own. What a mistake! She became obsessed with how she looked, and she powdered her face as white as snow and painted her lips as red as blood. Then she colored her hair as black as a raven's wing and changed her name to Snow White. She was not bad looking to begin with, but the way she made herself up was very strange. I prefer a more natural look, especially for a young girl.

Blanche would spend hours in front of my mirror ruining my expensive cosmetics. If I needed five minutes to fix my face, she would whine that I was being selfish. She also accused me of doing evil magic when I mixed lipstick colors! She neglected her studies and royal duties. If I offered her a cup of tea to calm her down she simply turned away from me. She was rude, sloppy, disobedient, and threatened to run away when she didn't get her way. I was worried for her safety.

Blanche liked to wander off into the forest, usually leaving her room a mess. She claimed she was gathering wildflowers, but she could never remember to bring any back. Sometimes she would be chased by the otherwise gentle castle dogs. For Blanche's own protection, I had my faithful huntsman watch over her. Thank goodness for him!

Deep in the woods one day, she discovered a run-down cottage that was home to seven strange little men. They had broken the law of the land and had been sentenced to hard manual labor in the mines as punishment. Obviously they were not suitable company for a young girl, but my stepdaughter wanted to stay, and she always did what she wanted. My huntsman was able to return and report her whereabouts to me. On his way back from tracking her, he had killed a wild boar. The whole castle enjoyed it for dinner.

The next morning I personally set out on my journey to save my stepdaughter. I knew Blanche would never agree to come home with me willingly, so I devised a plan and dressed up as an old peddler woman. I brought along an apple with a sleeping drug in it. I wasn't proud of what I was doing, but I was worried that those little men might harm her. She did not understand that they could be dangerous!

I arrived while the repulsive little men were working at the mine. Blanche was alone in the house, and I had no trouble getting her to take a bite of the apple. She collapsed before I could even get her out the door. The men came back and I had to run away and hide outside. Luckily, I could still hear what was being said.

"Oh, drat," said the ugliest little man. "She's dead. Now she can't cook or clean for us anymore."

"She was the best-looking girl we ever lured here," grunted another filthy outcast. "Let's put her in a glass coffin and charge admission if anyone wants to look at her."

There Blanche stayed, makeup intact, for quite awhile. One of the men always stood guard over her, so I was unable to rescue her. The men even charged people money to come see Blanche sleep.

One day a prince rode by. He was Prince Darming, the youngest son of a neighboring king. He was a failure at being a prince and had trouble slaying dragons, rescuing maidens, and doing anything else that princes are supposed to do. He thought that Blanche was very pretty and was determined to take the coffin home with him. Prince Darming and those horrible men had a terrible argument and fell on top of the coffin. The apple was dislodged and Princess Blanche woke up.

Here my story differs little from the one you've heard. Prince Darming and Blanche instantly fell in love and were married shortly thereafter. I am happy for them both—and it does go to show you that there is someone for everyone. They live in a dirty, run-down castle, but they seem content. Blanche still doesn't like me—but I leave her alone. For years she spread ridiculous rumors about me, but now, for the first time, I've had a chance to tell you the truth.

As far as my breaking the mirror and being killed— forget about it! I'm alive and well, and I use my makeup and my mirror every day. After all, it is certainly important for a queen to look nice. And when you hear about some-one, especially a stepmother who is wicked and mean, just remember—there's always another side to the story.

The End